Dedicated to the children of North Korea,
my awesome critique groups, and our Heavenly Father
who sends rice from heaven.

—TC

Dedicated to all the people of North Korea—especially the
children suffering from hunger and malnutrition.
I hope this book will have a positive impact on your lives.

—KJS

little bee books

An imprint of Bonnier Publishing USA
251 Park Avenue South, New York, NY 10010

Text copyright © 2018 by Tina Cho
Illustrations copyright © 2018 by Keum Jin Song

Manufactured in China   HUH 0518
First Edition   10 9 8 7 6 5 4 3 2 1
ISBN 978-1-4998-0682-3

Library of Congress Cataloging-in-Publication Data
Names: Cho, Tina M., author. | Song, Keum Jin, 1986- illustrator.
Title: Rice from Heaven / by Tina M. Cho; illustrated by Keum Jin Song.
Description: First edition. | New York, NY: Little Bee Books, [2018]
Summary: In South Korea, Yoori and her Appa, who grew up in North Korea, work with other villagers to send special
balloons to carry rice over the border into North Korea, where people are starving. | Identifiers: LCCN 2017038869
Subjects: | CYAC: Hunger—Fiction. | Charities—Fiction. | Korea (North)—Fiction. | Korea (South)—Fiction.
Classification: LCC PZ7.1.C5314 Ric 2018 | DDC [E]—dc23 | LC record available at https://lccn.loc.gov/2017038869

littlebeebooks.com
bonnierpublishingusa.com

Rice from Heaven

The Secret Mission to Feed North Koreans

by Tina Cho

illustrated by Keum Jin Song

little bee books

Out in the countryside, across a bridge, to an island blanketed with rice fields, Appa and I ride.

We reach a place where mountains become a wall. A wall so high, no one dares to climb.

Beyond that wall and across the sea live children

just like me, except they do not have enough food to eat.

North Korea is a gigantic, empty rice bowl with a government that does nothing to help its people.

Appa grew up there. Starving, he escaped down here to the south.

I am a little grain of rice. How can I help?

Appa says we can help in secret.

Tonight we will send special balloons carrying rice over the border to North Korea.

The sky darkens. We need a downpour to grow the grains of hope. From out of a shed, friends from church and I carry containers of rice to a launching pad. But the mission is interrupted.

Villagers glare and grumble. "Don't feed the enemy," children chant.

The hope in my heart withers like a dying rice stalk.

"Ignore them, Yoori," Appa says.

A mean-looking boy stomps up to us and raises his hands. I freeze with my feet planted firmly in the mud. And then words come spilling out of me like grains of rice tumbling out of a bag.

"We have to do this! We must help!
North Korean children have no rice.
They have no green fields like we do.
They eat grass and bark from trees."

Every eye stares at the boy. His face reddens. Teardrops and rain wash away the dirt of his actions. "They eat grass?" he asks. "I did not know that. I am very sorry. I will share the rice from my father's field."

Winds of change charge the air with quiet hope.

Appa hugs and showers me with kisses.
"You are my strong sunflower."

Drenched in her poncho, an older girl holding a rice bag moves close to me.

"Thank you for helping," she whispers. "I used to be one of those hungry children, eating once a day or not at all."

I bow low, but the hope in my heart grows tall.

We gather in groups to start our mission.
Air whishes into the balloon like a snake let
loose—slithering, impatient to be released—
until a rice bag is tied onto its tail.

With a little push, the balloon soars. Up, up, up.

The stars and moon hide under the rain clouds as two hundred balloons creep over the mountains like stealthy ninjas to fight hunger in the darkness of the night.

Under the glow from a streetlamp, I pray that North Korean soldiers do not spot the balloons. My heart is like a bubbly, steaming rice pot—full of hope.

I smile.

In the morning, hungry children will find rice from heaven.

Author's Note

By participating in this rice balloon project on May 2, 2016, I helped North Korean refugees who attended a church in Seoul send food to the country from which they escaped. For the safety of everyone involved, I can't disclose any names or whereabouts. North Korea warned against sending "propaganda" or any literature across the border. They don't want their citizens to know the outside world has freedom. Therefore, these balloons carried only rice.

Like the child in this story, I can only imagine the expressions of the North Korean adults and children who discovered this precious rice from heaven. Did they, in fact, receive it? We may never know. But I hope they felt the love and care that was sent to them.

Numbers

200 balloons launched

6 pounds, 9.8 ounces (3 kilograms) of rice tied to each balloon

Wind speed: 37.3 mph (60 km/h)

Estimated distance balloons traveled: 111.8 miles (180 km); the South Korean government's radar tracked the balloons

People who assisted: 40 or more

Location: about 3.1 miles (5 km) from the border

Time: balloons had enough hydrogen to stay airborne for 3 hours

Cost: $22,000 raised by churches and schoolchildren to fund the project

Total fed: unknown

Facts on Korea

In 918 AD, General Wang Geon established the Goryeo Dynasty, from which Korea gets its name. Goryeo means "high and clear," but there are many interpretations. Some believe it means "Land of High Mountains and Sparkling Streams," and others say it stands for "Land of the Morning Calm."

Guests remove their shoes when visiting someone's home in Korea.

In Korea, babies are considered one year old when they are born.

Kimchi, South Korea's favorite dish, is made with fermented vegetables such as cabbage.

Four is considered a very unlucky number in Korea. Some buildings don't have a fourth floor.

Politics of the Korean Peninsula

Korea was once a unified nation, but it is now divided into North and South Korea.

After World War II, Korea was occupied by other countries. The Soviet Union occupied northern Korea and the United States occupied southern Korea. The country was divided on whether to become a democratic and capitalist country or a Communist dictatorship. In 1948, with the backing of the US, South Korea became an independent country known as the Republic of Korea. The Soviet Union later declared a political leader in North Korea as having power over the entire Korean Peninsula. Tensions eventually led North Korea—with the help of China and the Soviet Union—to invade the south in 1950, starting what is now known as the Korean War. It lasted for three years and almost two million people died, including around 36,000 American soldiers. The Armistice Agreement of 1953 ended the fighting. However, neither North nor South Korea signed a peace treaty. Technically, this means that they are still at war.

After the fighting stopped, a demilitarized zone (DMZ), 155.3 miles (250 km) long and 2.5 miles (4 km) wide, was established as the new border between North and South Korea. The DMZ is intended to be a peaceful tract of land for ongoing peace talks, but both sides are heavily guarded by troops, and the area itself is dangerous and dotted with land mines planted by North Korea.

Facts on North Korea

- North Korea is a Communist state. That means the government owns the land, factories, and goods. Everyone is supposed to share the wealth this way. However, North Korea does not produce enough food for everybody.

- Citizens of North Korea have little access to basic resources such as food, health care, and electricity. More than half the population is malnourished and lives in extreme poverty.

- The government will only allow people to have short hair, and very few hairstyles are approved.

- North Korea has one of the largest militaries in the world.

- When students finish their education in North Korea, they are assigned jobs that will last for the rest of their lives. The government studies how many people are needed in each of their industries and assigns citizens jobs based on its findings.

- North Korea has a six-day workweek. The seventh day of the week is a "voluntary" extra day of work.

- People who speak out against the conditions are placed in labor camps, where the average workweek is 112 hours.

- North Korea has a Propaganda and Agitation Department, which controls all media communication. There are only three TV stations and they, alongside all the radio programming, air only government-approved material that promotes a positive view of the conditions in the country.

- There is a ban on cell phones, and the Internet is restricted to prevent communication with the outside world.

- There are many restrictions for visitors in North Korea. Cell phones must be handed over at the airport upon entry and are given back as visitors leave. Visitors are also escorted everywhere by a guide and must ask permission to take pictures.

- Some ways for citizens to leave the country are to flee north over the Chinese or Russian borders, through the DMZ into South Korea, or by boat to Japan. If escapees are found by the Chinese government, they are returned to North Korea.

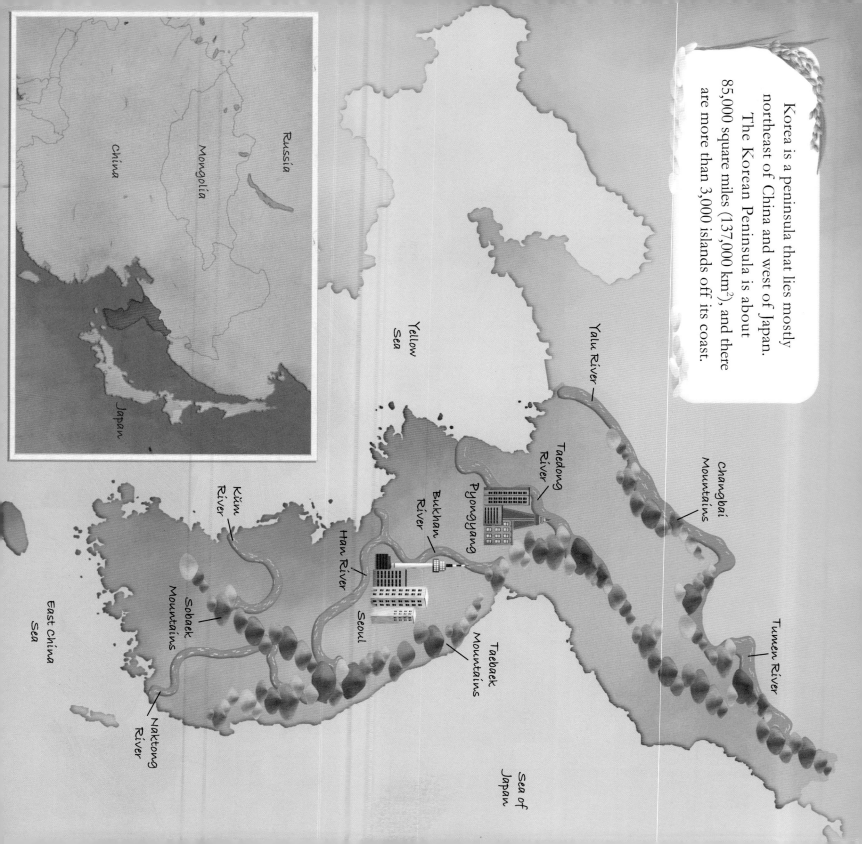

Korea is a peninsula that lies mostly northeast of China and west of Japan. The Korean Peninsula is about 85,000 square miles (137,000 km²), and there are more than 3,000 islands off its coast.

Russia

Mongolia

China

Japan

Yellow
Sea

Yalu River

Taedong
River

Pyongyang

Bukhan
River

Changbai
Mountains

Kŭm
River

Han River

Seoul

Sobaek
Mountains

Tumen River

Taebaek
Mountains

East China
Sea

Naktong
River

Sea of
Japan